MICHAEL GARLA

Miss Smith
and the
Haunted Library

PUFFIN BOOKS

An Imprint of Penguin Group (USA) Inc.

For my dad

PUFFIN BOOKS
Published by the Penguin Group
Penguin Young Readers Group, 345 Hudson Street, New York, New York 10014, U.S.A.
Penguin Group (Canada), 90 Eglinton Avenue East, Suite 700, Toronto, Ontario, Canada M4P 2Y3 (a division of Pearson Penguin Canada Inc.)
Penguin Books Ltd, 80 Strand, London WC2R 0RL, England
Penguin Ireland, 25 St Stephen's Green, Dublin 2, Ireland (a division of Penguin Books Ltd)
Penguin Group (Australia), 250 Camberwell Road, Camberwell, Victoria 3124, Australia (a division of Pearson Australia Group Pty Ltd)
Penguin Books India Pvt Ltd, 11 Community Centre, Panchsheel Park, New Delhi - 110 017, India
Penguin Group (NZ), 67 Apollo Drive, Rosedale, Auckland 0632, New Zealand (a division of Pearson New Zealand Ltd.)
Penguin Books (South Africa) (Pty) Ltd, 24 Sturdee Avenue, Rosebank, Johannesburg 2196, South Africa

Registered Offices: Penguin Books Ltd, 80 Strand, London WC2R 0RL, England

First published in the United States of America by Dutton, a division of Penguin Young Readers Group, 2009
Published by Puffin Books, a division of Penguin Young Readers Group, 2012

3 5 7 9 10 8 6 4 2

THE LIBRARY OF CONGRESS HAS CATALOGED THE DUTTON CHILDREN'S BOOKS EDITION AS FOLLOWS:
Garland, Michael.
Miss Smith and the haunted library / Michael Garland.
p. cm.
Summary: When Miss Smith brings her students to the public library, they not only meet Virginia Creeper, the librarian, but also a host of
frightening creatures that emerge from the pages of the "Incredible Storybook" as Ms. Creeper reads her favorite tales.
ISBN: 978-0-525-42139-9 (hc)
[1. Books and reading—Fiction. 2. Libraries—Fiction. 3. Teachers—Fiction. 4. Librarians—Fiction. 5. Magic—Fiction.] I. Title
PZ7.G18413 Mhh 2009
[E]—lcac
2008034219

Puffin Books ISBN 978-0-14-242122-2

Manufactured in China

ALWAYS LEARNING   PEARSON

Zack stared out of the classroom window at the dreary fall morning as he waited for his favorite teacher to arrive. Suddenly, Miss Smith burst through the door.

"Good morning, class! We're going to visit the library today. There is someone special who I want you to meet."

Zack smiled when Miss Smith picked up the *Incredible Storybook* before heading out the door.

The library was right down the block from school. Zack warily eyed the dark stone building as they walked single file up the sidewalk. The creaky door swung open and they tiptoed inside.

"Class," Miss Smith said, "this is our librarian, Virginia Creeper."

Zack stared in shock. Blue hair, pale skin, deep dark eyes—he hadn't been expecting this!

"Hello," Ms. Creeper said in a high-pitched squeaky voice. "How can I help you today?"

"This is the season for spooky stories. Do you have any suggestions?" Miss Smith asked.

"Oh yes," the librarian replied. "Quite a few! I might find some of them in your *Incredible Storybook*."

Miss Smith handed the book to Virginia Creeper. The librarian opened it and said, "I'll just read a little from my favorite scary stories."

Ms. Creeper began to read about a dark, haunted wood. Zack shivered. Then, with a thunder of hooves, the Headless Horseman leaped out of the book!

The children's mouths hung open in disbelief. Virginia Creeper started reading again, and the Hound of the Baskervilles pounced from the book. More reading added the clinking and rattling of chains as Marley's Ghost appeared.

New stories brought out the Hunchback of Notre Dame, Frankenstein, and Count Dracula!

The class started to cling to Miss Smith. The great black horse snorted and stomped his hooves. Frankenstein groaned, but Virginia Creeper just kept on reading as a flock of ghosts flew from the book.

When Captain Hook and the Wicked Witch of the West entered the room, Zack wondered if he should run for the door.

The scary creatures were crowding the room, but that didn't stop Virginia Creeper from reading. Rumpelstiltskin, The Queen of Hearts, and the Big Bad Wolf squeezed in among the others. Zack looked up and saw the giant from Jack and the Beanstalk bump his head on the ceiling.

Next, the room was filled with eerie sounds of whiffling and burbling. Virginia Creeper read on as the flaming-eyed Jabberwocky arrived in a puff of smoke.

Then the strangest thing happened. Virginia Creeper stopped reading and started to pass out cookies and apple cider to the children and the characters. The mood changed. To Zack's amazement, a party started!

All the creatures seemed happy to be at the library. The Headless Horseman gave horsey rides and the kids lined up! Someone brought out a ball and played fetch with the Hound of the Baskervilles. Dracula told jokes. The giant gently picked up some kids and lifted them high in the air.

Everyone was enjoying the fun. The characters didn't seem so scary now!

Virginia Creeper's happy smile suddenly changed to a worried frown when she looked out the window and saw the seniors' book club coming up the walk.

"Oh my," said Ms. Creeper, "I almost forgot. It's time for the book club! They can't see this! It will give the seniors such a fright."

"Go and tidy up while I stall them at the door!" the librarian told Miss Smith.

Virginia Creeper blocked the impatient readers from entering while Miss Smith ran around in a tizzy. She picked up overturned chairs and straightened the book shelves.

Outside, the seniors were getting grouchy, but inside, the kids and the characters had become too silly to notice.

"Can I help?" Zack asked Miss Smith.

She handed the *Incredible Storybook* to Zack.

"Remember," Miss Smith said, "we have to finish each story so that the characters will go back into the book. Read the last page of each tale, while I deal with *this mess!*"

Zack opened up the book and quickly finished all the stories. One by one, the characters went back into the *Incredible Storybook.*

The puzzled book club burst into the room just as Zack finished the last page.

"Okay, class, it's time to check out your books," Miss Smith said. She guided the class toward the big front desk.

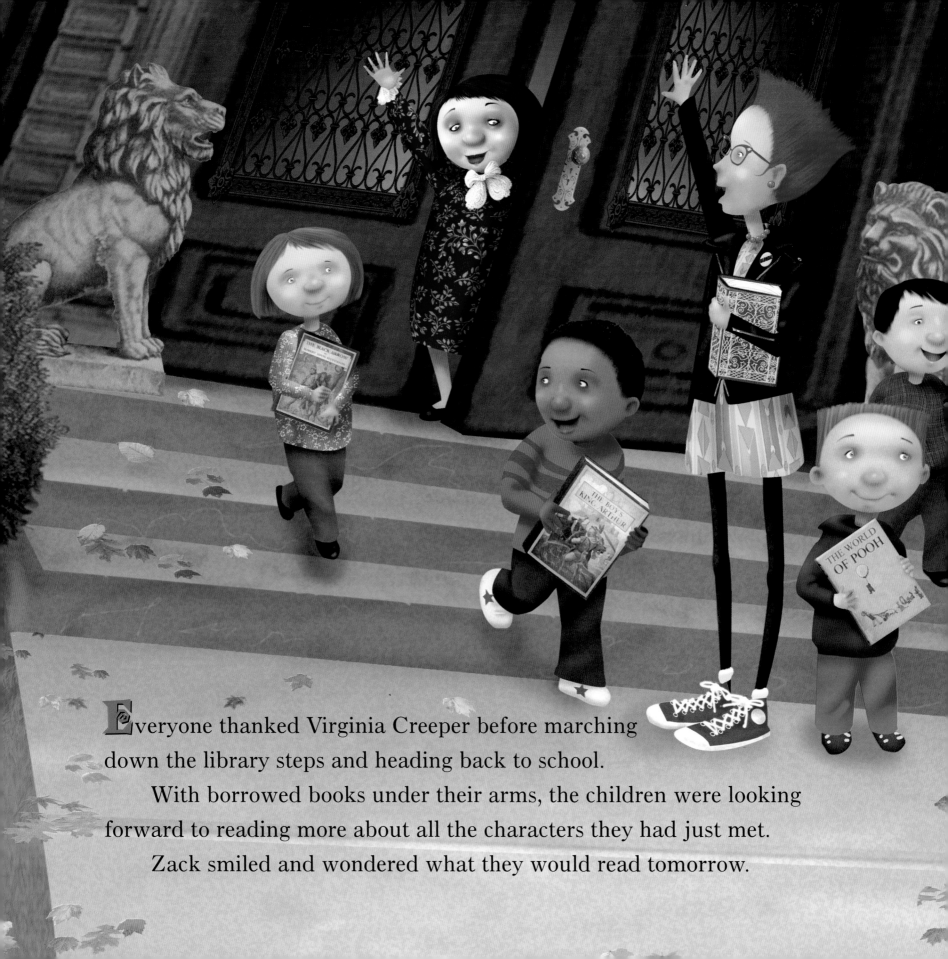

Everyone thanked Virginia Creeper before marching
down the library steps and heading back to school.

With borrowed books under their arms, the children were looking
forward to reading more about all the characters they had just met.

Zack smiled and wondered what they would read tomorrow.